W9-AVN-717

The
Tiara
Club

No longer property of
Long Beach Public Library

VIVIAN FRENCH

The Tiara Club

✦ AT SILVER TOWERS ✦

Princess Charlotte
AND THE
Enchanted Rose

ILLUSTRATED BY SARAH GIBB

KATHERINE TEGEN BOOKS
An Imprint of HarperCollins*Publishers*

The Tiara Club at Silver Towers:

Princess Charlotte and the Enchanted Rose

Text copyright © 2007 by Vivian French

Illustrations copyright © 2007 by Sarah Gibb

Library of Congress Cataloging-in-Publication Data is available.

ISBN-10: 0-06-112442-7 (trade bdg.)

ISBN-13: 978-0-06-112442-6 (trade bdg.)

ISBN-10: 0-06-112441-9 (pbk.)

ISBN-13: 978-0-06-112441-9 (pbk.)

Typography by Amy Ryan

First U.S. edition, 2007

09 10 11 12 13 CG/CW 10 9 8 7 6 5 4

For Princess Charlotte's mum,
Queen Catriona, with love
—V.F.

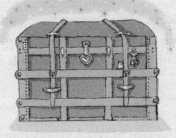

For Julie, with love
—S.G.

The Royal Palace Academy
for the Preparation of Perfect Princesses
(Known to our students as "The Princess Academy")

OUR SCHOOL MOTTO:
*A Perfect Princess always thinks of others before herself,
and is kind, caring, and truthful.*

Silver Towers offers a complete education for
Tiara Club princesses with emphasis on
selected outings. The curriculum includes:

Fans and Curtseys

A visit to Witch Windlespin
(Royal herbalist, healer, and maker of magic potions)

Problem Prime Ministers

A visit to the Museum of Royal Life
(Students will be well protected from the Poisoned Apple)

Our principal, Queen Samantha Joy, is present
at all times, and students are in the excellent care of
the school Fairy Godmother, Fairy Angora.

OUR RESIDENT STAFF & VISITING EXPERTS INCLUDE:

LADY ALBINA MacSPLINTER *(School Secretary)*

CROWN PRINCE DANDINO *(Field Trips)*

QUEEN MOTHER MATILDA *(Etiquette, Posture, and Poise)*

FAIRY G. *(Head Fairy Godmother)*

We award tiara points to encourage our
Tiara Club princesses toward the next level.
All princesses who win enough points at Silver
Towers will attend the Silver Ball, where they
will be presented with their Silver Sashes.

Silver Sash Tiara Club princesses are invited
to return to Ruby Mansions, our exclusive
residence for Perfect Princesses, where they may
continue their education at a higher level.

PLEASE NOTE:

Princesses are expected to arrive
at the Academy with a *minimum* of:

TWENTY BALL GOWNS
*(with all necessary hoops,
petticoats, etc.)*

TWELVE DAY-DRESSES

SEVEN GOWNS
*suitable for garden parties
and other special daytime
occasions*

TWELVE TIARAS

DANCING SHOES
five pairs

VELVET SLIPPERS
three pairs

RIDING BOOTS
two pairs

*Cloaks, muffs, stoles, gloves,
and other essential
accessories, as required*

Good day, dear Tiara Club Princess. Princess Charlotte sends you greetings!

Oh, it's no good. I don't think I'll ever be able to talk like a real princess. But I'm so pleased you're coming to Silver Towers at the Royal Palace Academy with me and Katie, Daisy, Alice, Sophia, and Emily—it'll be such fun! We'll float around being Perfect Princesses, and every day will be just perfect . . . although my first day wasn't perfect at all!

Chapter One

*I*t was my first day ever at Silver Towers!

I was so excited I could hardly breathe. I'd started packing weeks and weeks before, and I'd read the letter from the principal about a million times.

The
Tiara Club
at Silver Towers

Dear Princess Charlotte,

We look forward very much to welcoming you to Silver Towers, where you will continue your education at the Royal Palace Academy for the Preparation of Perfect Princesses. Please note that there will be a Royal Reception at 6:00 pm, and dress accordingly.

With all good wishes,
Queen Samantha Joy

P.S. A map of Silver Towers is enclosed. Please make your way to the Grand Entrance on arrival.

I kept pinching myself as our coach rattled along the road. I'd been dreaming for so long that I was a proper Tiara Club Princess at Silver Towers—and now I was nearly there.

My trunks were on the seat beside me, and I had a beautiful new dress for the Royal Reception. It was pale violet silk, with the sweetest little matching shoes with real pearl buckles, so I really did feel almost pretty when I wore it. (My hair's rather plain, and my nose is very ordinary.) And I was longing to see Katie, Daisy, Alice, Sophia, and Emily.

I'd missed them so much over the holidays! Of course, we'd sent plenty of letters by Royal Messenger, but now we were going to be together again.

When we finally turned in

through the twirly silver gates, I bounced from one side of the coach to the other, trying to see everything at once. The silver towers were so romantic! Even though it was a gray day, they were still shining and the

tops reached right up to the clouds.

We drove into a huge courtyard, and the coach stopped.

"Is this the place, Your Royal Highness?" the footman asked.

I fished around in my bag for the map—and it wasn't there. I'd forgotten it, even though Mom and Dad had reminded me about a hundred times before they went off on their Royal Tour. I could see an enormous doorway, though. That *had* to be the Grand Entrance, so I said, "Yes! This is it! Thank you!" The coachman piled my trunks by the step, and there I was—standing outside my new school.

Rat-a-tat-tat! I grabbed the knocker and banged on the door with a flourish, but there was no answer. And I suddenly noticed how quiet it was. Surely there should be other princesses arriving by now.

I began to feel just a teeny bit anxious. *Could I be in the wrong place after all?* I didn't quite see how I could be, because all the signs saying SILVER TOWERS: MAIN ENTRANCE had pointed to the courtyard where I was standing. I decided to go and check—just to be sure. I could see another archway in the wall beyond the front door, so I ran over to look. It was beginning to rain, but I didn't pay any attention.

Oooops!

I felt so stupid. There was another sign pointing through the arch, and in the distance I could see

rows of coaches. They were standing outside a huge silver doorway that was so amazing I realized I must have gone to the back door. Even though there was nobody around to see me, I turned bright red. If only I'd remembered the map!

I crept a little farther through the arch, and something caught my eye—a rose! A real rose! It was lying in a muddy puddle, so I picked it up. And then I saw another, and another, and by the time I'd picked them all up, I had a whole bunch. I was just wondering why they'd been thrown away when I heard the rumble of wheels behind me, and my heart jumped. *Could it be my friends?* It sounded like a big coach, and Princess Sophia's coach was huge. I swung around to take a look—and stared!

The grandest coach I'd ever seen in my entire life was bowling toward me. It was covered in so many glittering jewels, I had to rub my eyes. It slowed down as it reached the archway, and I saw a snooty-looking girl peering at me from the window. A voice said, "Look, Gruella! There's a strange, dirty girl outside!" I had a quick glimpse of another sneering face, and it was exactly the same!

And then they went through the arch and out the other side. I glared after them. They were so rude! I looked down at my beautiful traveling dress, which wasn't beautiful anymore. It was dripping wet and

covered in muddy splatters.

I nearly burst into tears. I'd thought being at Silver Towers was going to be fabulous and lovely, and it wasn't. It was absolutely horrible.

Chapter Two

I put the roses on the back doorstep, sat down next to my trunks, and stared at my sopping shoes. I could imagine how terrible I'd look walking in through that huge silver doorway.

"Dear Charlotte! What are you doing?"

I knew that voice! I was so relieved, I burst into tears—tears of happiness. A gigantic golden coach had stopped a short distance away, and Sophia was hanging out of the window. Princess Daisy, Princess Emily, and Princess Katie were trying to look around her, and they all seemed really worried as they stared at me.

"Everything's gone wrong!" I cried. "I came to the wrong entrance and I'm completely soaked and my dress is ruined!"

The next minute they were

running toward me.

"You poor thing!" Emily said.
"You're drenched!"

"Quick!" Katie caught my hand.
"Get into the coach!"

Daisy grabbed my other hand, and we dashed through the rain. We landed in Sophia's coach in a heap, and hugged one another. It

was so good to see them!

"Oh, look!" Katie began to giggle. "We're almost as wet as you are! But how did you get so muddy?"

"I was trying to find the front door," I said, "and this sparkly coach went right past me. It must have splashed me." I suddenly remembered the girls inside. "There were two princesses I've never seen before. I think they were twins."

"Twins?" Emily's eyes lit up. "That'll be fun!"

"They didn't look very fun," I said. "One girl said I was dirty."

Sophia looked horrified. "You

mean they saw you and they didn't stop to help you?"

Daisy frowned. "That's terrible. Princesses should always help people."

"It doesn't matter," I said. I was so

happy to be with my friends, I didn't mind anymore. "Do you know when Princess Alice is arriving?"

"She was just behind us," Katie said. She scrambled onto the backseat and peered through the

window. "Here she is! Just coming into the courtyard, and she's stopping!"

The next thing I knew, Alice was leaning out of the window of her coach, and Sophia was telling her how she'd found me. A second later, Alice hopped in with us.

"Grandfather's telling his coachman to collect your luggage," she told me. "We'll arrive together—

goodness, you're soaked!"

"I know," I said. "And it's my fault." And then a totally terrible thought struck me. Would anybody ever believe we were princesses? Our hair was a disaster, our dresses were dripping, and our shoes were covered in mud. My stomach tied

itself into knots. "What if they won't let us in?"

"They'll let Alice in," Daisy said. "She looks perfect!"

Daisy was right. Alice had on a

beautiful blue velvet dress and forget-me-not blue satin slippers.

Alice looked at us and grinned a wicked grin. "Wait!" she ordered, and before we could stop her, she

was outside, dancing in the rain. She didn't come back until she was just as wet as the rest of us.

"There!" she said. "If they don't want us, at least we can all be together. Look—my grandfather's coach is moving on. It's time to make our grand entrance at Silver Towers!"

Chapter Three

My heart was thumping as Sophia's coach drew up outside the massive front door. There was a red carpet walkway, and pageboys were waiting with umbrellas. When they saw us getting out of the coach, they had to try really hard not to laugh, and that made Alice and Katie giggle. A moment later, we were all laughing. We hurried along the carpet and in through the door. Inside, it was amazing!

The hallway was enormous, and

rows and rows of huge, glittery chandeliers positively dazzled us. We tried not to stare, but it was very hard not to. After the gloom of the rain outside, it looked so sparkly and beautiful, and it was

wonderfully warm, too.

"Welcome—oh! Oh! *Oh! Never* have I seen princesses arrive in such a state!"

The tall, thin teacher standing by the door looked at us in the most reprimanding way as she checked

our names on her clipboard.

"You are all in Silver Rose Room. I shall order your trunks to be taken there immediately, and you will change out of those *disgusting* dresses. Queen Samantha Joy will be making her formal speech at the Royal Reception at six o'clock precisely, and you must not be late!"

And although Alice's sweet grandfather tried to explain what had happened, the teacher took us away as if we were babies. She hardly let Alice kiss him good-bye, and she kept tutting at us all the way up the white marble stairs.

"Now," she snapped, as she opened a door and marched us through. "Be quick! And take six minus tiara points each." The door slammed shut, and she was gone.

We sank down on our beds and stared at each other.

"Minus tiara points?" I gasped.

"Didn't I tell you?" Alice said. "When my big sis was here she had tons of minus points. She only just had enough to go on to Ruby Mansions." She picked up a pillow and thumped it. "Just before I left

home she told me we'd have a huge surprise on our first day, but this is a horrible surprise!"

I looked at her, amazed. Alice is hardly ever upset.

"Maybe something good will happen soon," I said hopefully.

"Maybe." Alice still sounded annoyed. "It'll have to be very good to make up for minus tiara points."

I was beginning to feel uncomfortable. If I hadn't been so stupid, I'd have gone to the right door, and then I wouldn't have gotten wet, and then my friends wouldn't have gotten wet either, and we wouldn't have gotten any minus tiara points!

"I'm not sure if I'm going to like it here," Katie sighed, and Daisy nodded.

"We'd better get unpacked," Emily said gloomily, "or we'll be in

even more trouble."

"At least we're all in the same dormitory." I was trying hard to be cheerful.

"But it's so plain." Katie made a face. "Look! Washed-out pink walls, and one tiny little rug!"

"It doesn't look like our old Rose Room," Daisy said wistfully.

Sophia suddenly sat up straighter. "Mmmm . . . I can *smell* roses," she said.

We looked around and there, on top of my luggage, were the roses I'd picked up and left on the step. The coachman must have thought I'd brought them with me.

"That's strange," I said as I looked at them. "They were all muddy when I found them."

Alice suddenly smiled. "Maybe they're magic!"

"They're beautiful!" Sophia picked one up and sniffed it. "Oh! That's just heavenly!"

Then I had a totally brilliant idea.

"I'll share them with the Rose Room!" I said. "Roses for the Rose Roomers—my very special friends!"

Chapter Four

*I*t wasn't quite six o'clock when we hurried down the stairs. The dormitory looked so much better by the time we shut the door behind us; I'd put roses on everybody's bedside tables, and they made the room almost glow. We all felt better too—even Alice was cheerful again. As I did my pearl buckles up, I began to think maybe everything was going to be all right after all.

When we found the Throne Room, it was full of princesses.

They were sitting in rows on white satin chairs, and we sneaked into the back as quietly as we could. We could see Princess Freya, and Princess Jemima, and loads of our other friends, but there was no sign of horrible Princess Perfecta or

nasty Princess Floreen. I heaved a sigh of relief. They'd been so mean before!

And then I saw the twins. They were sitting on the other side of the aisle from us, and they were sneering as if they thought I was really, really, really horrible.

"Hey, Diamonde," one said

loudly. "It's that dirty girl again!"

But before the other twin could answer, there was a fanfare of golden trumpets, and the most wonderful procession of beautifully dressed queens and kings paraded past us and up to the thrones in front of the velvet curtains.

"Wow!" I gasped, and then I clutched at Alice's arm. "Look," I whispered. "It's Fairy G. and Fairy Angora."

And it was! Dear, dear Fairy G., our Fairy Godmother from before, was stomping along at the back of the procession. Beside her floated Fairy Angora, whom we'd met just before we'd got into the Tiara Club. She was so beautiful you could never forget her—even if she wasn't very good at magic spells.

"Fairy Angora looks terrible!" Alice hissed in my ear.

She was right. Fairy Angora was very pale, and she kept blowing her nose.

I was about to say, "Maybe she's got a cold," but I suddenly saw our new principal frowning at us. She looked—I couldn't think of the right word, and then I thought, "Magnificent, but so scary!"

"Good evening to you all," she said, and her voice was lovely—

very deep and warm. I began to feel a tiny bit better, although she was still looking stern. "I am delighted to welcome such a splendid gathering of princesses to Silver Towers. I hope this will be a truly wonderful experience for each one of you, and that we will be able to congratulate you all on winning your Silver Sashes and moving on to Ruby Mansions when the time comes."

Queen Samantha Joy paused. "We are extremely pleased that we have been able to appoint Fairy Angora as the school Fairy Godmother. Of course, some of you will have met her before.

Unfortunately, I must bring a serious matter to your attention. Sometime between driving through the gates and arriving at school, she

lost a very valuable and magic item. A search has taken place, but nothing has been found. I cannot imagine any of my princesses would be responsible, but I have to ask. Have any of you seen a bunch of enchanted roses?"

Chapter Five

I wanted to die. My heart was thumping so hard I thought everyone must have heard it. I felt awful.

I stood up, but before I could say a word the twins leaped into the aisle. One of them shouted, "*We* saw someone sneaking around with a bunch of roses. Didn't we, Gruella?"

Princess Gruella nodded. "And *we* know who she is, don't we, Diamonde?"

The Throne Room was suddenly full of rustlings and murmurings. "It's *her*!" Princess Diamonde pointed straight at me. And she and Gruella smirked triumphantly.

I looked at their grinning faces, and I ran. The one thing I'm really good at is running, and I absolutely tore out of the Throne Room, up the stairs, and into the Rose Room. I seized the roses and dashed back as fast as I could go. I was puffing hard, but I managed to walk steadily up to Queen Samantha Joy and curtsied.

"Please," I said, "*please* excuse me. I found them in the mud."

And then I curtsied again, and I only wobbled a little bit. "I'm so very sorry—"

And I had to stop. If I'd said anything else I'd have burst into tears. I gulped loudly and stared at my feet as I waited to be told I had to leave Silver Towers.

There was a moment of complete and utter silence, and then Fairy Angora spoke.

"Would the Princesses Gruella and Diamonde please come here?"

Sophia said afterward that she just knew the twins thought they were going to be told how good

they were. They waltzed in between the rows of chairs as if they were collecting a million tiara points.

"Now," Fairy Angora said, and she sounded so sweet and kind I felt a zillion times worse. "Princess Charlotte, may I see the roses?"

I swallowed hard and held them out.

It was so odd! They looked even better than they had before. Each rose had a sparkling silver dewdrop deep in its velvet petals, and the scent almost made me dizzy. And I suddenly realized Alice had been right. They *were* magic.

Fairy Angora looked at them,

and her smile was amazing. I took a little sideways peek at Fairy G., and she was smiling too.

"Aha," Fairy Angora said. "Just as I thought." She took a rose and handed it to Gruella. Gruella shrieked and dropped it at once.

"It's got thorns!" she squealed.

"Don't touch it, Diamonde!"

"Don't tell me what to do, Gruella!" Diamonde snapped. She grabbed at the poor flower, and at once the petals lost their color and drooped miserably.

"You see?" Fairy Angora said gently. She tucked the rose back

into the bunch I was still holding—
and it was suddenly perfect again!

There was a loud "Ooooooh!"
from everyone—even Queen
Samantha Joy.

Fairy G. beamed, and her eyes
twinkled as she stepped forward.

"Enchanted roses always know

when someone has a truly kind heart," she boomed in her extraordinarily loud voice. "And also"—she gave Gruella and Diamonde a frosty stare—"when they mean to be unkind."

And Gruella and Diamonde rushed back to their seats, blushing a deep red.

"Well done, Fairy Godmother Angora! And well said, Fairy G.!" Queen Samantha Joy began to laugh, and it was such a wonderful deep chuckle I couldn't help laughing too. She bent down and pinched my cheek.

"Poor little Charlotte! What a

beginning to your time at Silver
Towers. Why don't I give ten tiara
points to everyone from Silver Rose
Room to cheer you up."

And I could hardly believe it,

but my magnificent new principal winked at me! "And now," she went on, "give Fairy Angora the roses and run back to your seat. It's time we got ready for the Rose Petal Ball."

Chapter Six

We'd never ever guessed there was to be a ball that evening! We watched in amazement as Fairy Angora gently brushed the walls of the Throne Room with the enchanted roses, so they were instantly draped with the palest pink

satin covered in swathes of shimmer-
ing silver netting. Strings and strings
of twinkly pink flower-petal lights

looped themselves across the ceiling,
and music floated through the air
in the most mysterious way. It was

utterly and completely magical!

Then Queen Samantha Joy began dancing with Fairy G., and we couldn't help laughing as they

sailed around the room together. They looked so funny! The grown-ups sat on the chairs and chatted while Alice, Katie, Emily, Daisy,

Sophia, and I danced and danced until we could hardly keep our eyes open.

As we walked slowly up the stairs to our dormitory, Emily asked, "Was that the surprise your sister meant, Alice? The Rose Petal Ball?"

Alice yawned. "I don't know. It's been nothing but surprises ever since we got here."

I skipped a little as we opened our door. "I like surprises—well, I like the nice ones."

"That's good," Sophia said. She was standing right in front of me, and I could see her eyes were wide. "Come and look!"

And we stared and stared. On each of our beds was a heap of crimson velvet heart-shaped cushions and a scatter of rose petals.

"Wow!" I gasped, "wow!" And as we snuggled down, I just knew that being at Silver Towers was going to be the happiest time in my life, and I'm so glad you're here too.

What happens next?

FIND OUT IN

Princess Katie
∽ AND THE ∾
Mixed-up Potion

Hello, and how are you? Thank you SO much for being at Silver Towers with us . . . Oh! You do know who we are, don't you? I'm Princess Katie, and I share the Silver Rose Room with the Princesses Charlotte, Alice, Emily, Daisy, and Sophia. We're all trying really hard to win our Silver Sashes—but it's hard work getting tiara points, especially when those HORRIBLE twins are around. . . .

You are cordially invited
to the Royal Princess Academy

Follow the adventures of your special princess friends
as they try to earn enough points to join the Tiara Club.

Katherine Tegen Books
An Imprint of HarperCollinsPublishers